ELLA'S BIG CHANCE

A Fairy Tale Retold

Shirley Hughes

THE BODLEY HEAD

LONDON

ELLA'S BIG CHANCE

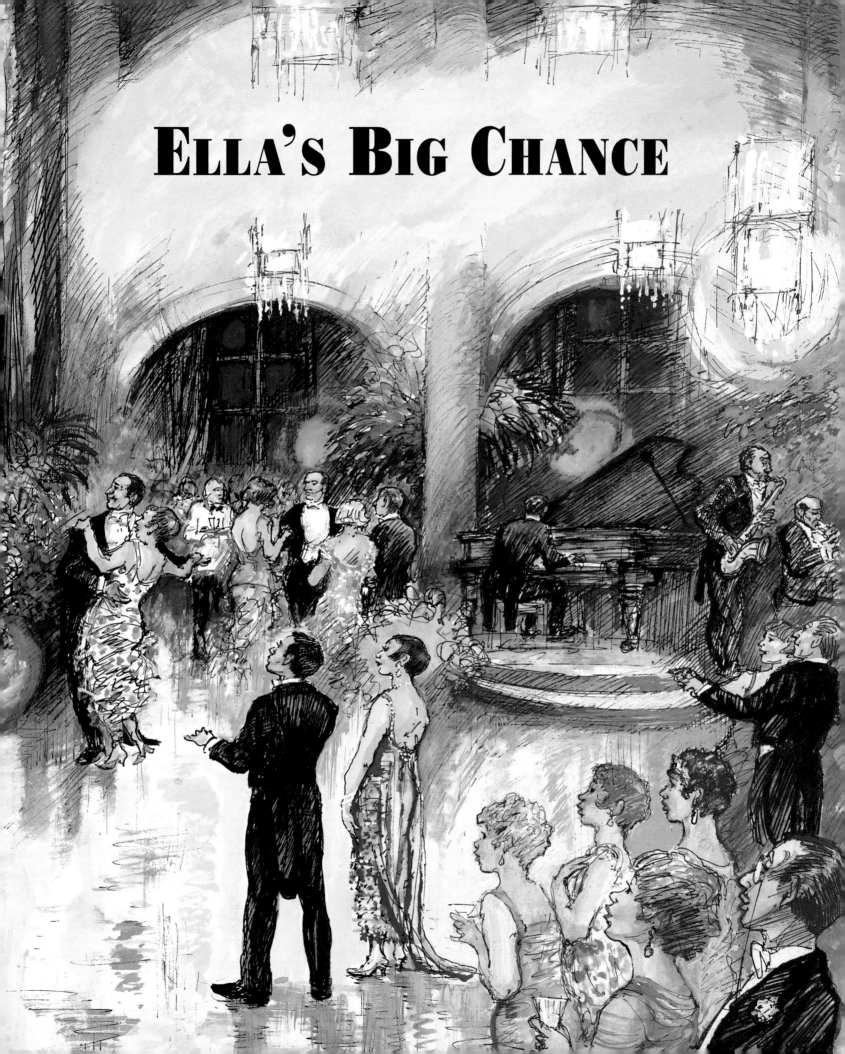

Mr Cinders kept a little dress shop in a quiet but elegant part of town. People came from far and near to buy clothes from him because he made such lovely things.

His wife had died, leaving him with one daughter, a red-haired girl called Ella whom he dearly loved. He taught her about silks and wools and satins and how to coax them into coats and dresses. So, by and by, she became as good a dressmaker as he was, if not better.

Mr Cinders and Ella ran the shop together with the help of a lively lad called Buttons. This was his name because he wore a short jacket with three rows of shiny buttons on the front. He also wore trousers with a gold stripe down the sides and a round cap set on at a jaunty angle.

Buttons polished the glass on the front of the shop until it shone, and opened the door for the customers. In the afternoon he bicycled about the town delivering parcels and boxes.

In between times, whenever he could, he would chat to Ella while she was busy sewing. He could always make her laugh, even if her mouth was full of pins.

All went on happily until the terrible day when Mr Cinders decided to marry again. His new wife seemed to pop up from nowhere like a sharp-eyed, expensively dressed jack-in-the-box. Still worse, she had two daughters of her own, and very beautiful creatures they were too.

Madame Renée was her name and she soon changed things at the shop. She had everything redecorated and enlarged the salon. She put advertisements in all the smart magazines to increase trade. This meant that Ella and her father and Buttons had to work harder than ever.

Neither Madame Renée nor her daughters knew how to sew. Instead, Madame Renée managed everything and her two daughters, Ruby and Pearl, were models.

They strolled languidly up and down, showing off the clothes to the customers.

The shop was now a huge success, and all might have been well if Ruby and Pearl had not behaved so spitefully to Ella. They called her names like Podge and Carrots and expected her to wait on them as they lazed about on cushioned divans.

They kept Ella working such long hours at her sewing machine that she hardly had a moment to herself. If she fell asleep at the workroom table they woke her up and scolded her. Now she no longer had a room of her own. She shared a cramped basement full of cuttings and rolls of cloth with the old grey cat.

Mr Cinders was far too much under his wife's thumb to interfere. Ella could tell by his face that he knew things were going badly wrong. But he seemed suddenly to have grown old and could only remain silent as his stepdaughters preened themselves in the beautiful gowns which Ella had made, while the only thing she, his own daughter, had to wear was a shabby black dress.

The one person who took Ella's side was loyal Buttons. These days he hated working at the shop but he stayed in the job for her sake. He often exchanged sharp words with Ruby and Pearl when Madame Renée was out of earshot. Privately he called them a couple of puffed-up, dressed-up, made-up, stuck-up, brainless parakeets.

Whenever he could, he would slip down to Ella's basement and try to cheer her up. He would strum his guitar and coaxed her to sing the songs that reminded them of happier times.

Sometimes they even danced together, two little figures in the moonlit room, moving softly in and out among the bales of cloth.

The most important customer who came to the shop was the Duchess of Arc, a lady of enormous wealth. She always arrived in her luxurious car and swept into the salon, swathed in furs and superb diamonds.

Then how Madame Renée fussed and flattered and commanded Ruby and Pearl to parade all the best gowns that Ella's clever fingers had created.

Imagine the excitement when one day an invitation arrived from the Duchess announcing that a grand ball was to be held at her villa in honour of her only son, the Duke of Arc, lately returned from abroad. All the ladies and gentlemen of any importance in the neighbourhood were asked to attend.

At once Ruby and Pearl began to vie with one another in a very jealous manner about what they intended to wear.

The shop was thrown into a fever of activity. There was such a posturing in front of mirrors and draping of silks and satins, such a confusion of feathers and jewellery, that the place began to look like an Aladdin's cave. Ella was set to work night and day to make their dresses, and a very good job she made of it.

'Will I be going to the ball too?' she asked when every last stitch was finished to perfection. Ruby and Pearl merely sniggered rudely at this.

'You? Go to the ball?' they said. 'No chance, Carrots, you're far too shabby. Besides, you couldn't possibly get into any of the dresses!'

'I think you're mean!' cried Ella. 'The invitation was for all of us!'

'Good heavens, child, surely you can understand that it would never do for us to be seen with someone like you!' was all they replied.

Ella was too proud to cry.

On the evening of the ball she helped them to arrange their hair and put on their dresses, pretending that she didn't care. When at last the hired limousine arrived, Ruby, in shades of red, Pearl, in palest pink, and Madame Renée, all a-glitter in black, swept out without even saying goodbye.

Only Mr Cinders lingered for a moment to kiss his daughter goodnight with a sad look which said: 'You see how it is. There's nothing I can do.'

Then they were gone.

Ella went slowly down-stairs to her dreary basement room and sat down on the floor among the snippets of cloth. She gathered the old grey cat onto her lap. 'I'll bet it's a horrible stuck-up affair anyway,' she whispered. 'But, oh, puss, I would love to have seen it all!' And a few hot tears fell onto his fur.

Just then there came a soft tap on the door and there was Buttons.

'So they wouldn't let you go, Ella,' he said. 'Downright spiteful, I call it. You're twice as pretty as they are. But never mind. I'm cooking bacon and eggs in the kitchen. Come on, we'll have a party of our own.'

In the kitchen Buttons put on an apron and got busy at the stove while Ella fetched the milk from the doorstep.

Just as she stepped out a strange lady stepped in, carrying a fancy umbrella.

'I am your Fairy Godmother,' she told Ella, briskly peeling off her gloves. 'It's my job to see that you go to the ball, so don't let's waste time. First, I must think how to get you there. Come outside, both of you, and bring the cat.'

Outside in the street the Fairy Godmother looked about her thoughtfully. There was nothing in sight which looked very promising as transport – only Buttons' old delivery bicycle which was propped up against the railings. But when the Fairy Godmother tapped it lightly with her folded umbrella it instantly turned into a large, grey, gleaming limousine.

Then just another tap on the old cat's head transformed him at once into a smart chauffeur, dressed in an immaculate dove-grey uniform, who stood by the open door.

Ella clasped Buttons' hand tightly in amazement.

'But I can't go to the ball,' she cried. 'Not like this. I look terrible.'

The Fairy Godmother sketched a shape in the air with her umbrella and at once Ella was dressed in a ball dress as light as a silver cobweb, glittering all over with crystal beads, which fitted her perfectly. She wore a tiny silk hat to hide her hair in case she was recognized, silver stockings and – tap! tap! – a pair of little glass slippers on her feet.

'Oh, Ella!' was all Buttons could say. He had never seen her look so elegant.

'You are to be home by the last stroke of midnight,' the Fairy Godmother told Ella. 'The magic only lasts until then. After that it's back to normal.'

'I won't forget,' cried Ella excitedly as she stepped into the car.

'Enjoy yourself, Ella!' Buttons called after her as she was driven away. Ella waved from the back window of the car until she was out of sight.

When Buttons looked round, the Fairy Godmother seemed to have gone too. 'Now there's nobody left to share the bacon and eggs, not even the cat,' he said aloud. And he went back, all alone, into the shop.

Ella caused quite a stir when she arrived at the ball. None of the guests had seen such a striking girl before or one who was so beautifully dressed. And when the Duchess of Arc herself presented Ella to her son, gossip rustled around the ballroom like a hot wind through dry grass. But nobody, not even Ella's family, guessed who she was.

The Duke was dark-haired, grey-eyed and very, very handsome. He asked Ella to dance and they took the floor. All the other guests fell away.

Ella found she was not in the least over-awed by him. They chatted and laughed as they glided and spun, two-stepped, quick-stepped, fox-trotted and tangoed in perfect time together.

In the supper room, lit by a hundred paper lanterns, the Duke had eyes only for her.

He had never met a girl
like her. She was so full of
life, so ready to enjoy
herself, compared with the
cool, languid beauties of his
own circle.

Of course, Ella did not
notice the time. Why should
she? She was having too
much fun. She was waltzing
in the Duke's arms when
the clock began to strike
midnight. What a terrible
shock for Ella!

One . . . two . . . three . . .

'I've got to go!' she
muttered, diving across the
ballroom and scattering the
astonished dancers.

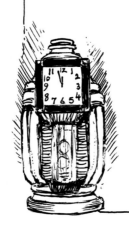

Four . . . five . . . six . . .

She ran out of the French windows and down the many marble steps to the garden below.

'Stay, stay with me a moment!' cried the Duke, hurrying after her. But Ella was fleeing away into the darkness.

Seven . . . eight . . . nine . . .

'I don't even know your name!' he called. All he heard was the faint clang of the iron gates as they closed behind her.

On the steps, at his feet, lay a little glass slipper.

Ten . . . eleven . . . twelve!

The last stroke came just as Ella reached the big grey limousine with the chauffeur holding wide the door. In an instant all that remained was Buttons' battered bicycle lying in the middle of the road. Beside it was the old grey cat with his coat standing on end, looking extremely put out.

Ella looked down at her black dress. It seemed shabbier than ever. But somehow she found she was holding in her hand one little glass slipper.

She put it into her pocket and picked up the bicycle. Sadly, she had never learned to ride one so she had to push it all the way back to the shop, limping along the road in her bare feet.

The cat, refusing a lift in the basket, stalked off crossly into the night to make his own way home.

The next day Ruby and Pearl did not bother to get out of bed until the afternoon, when they finally appeared, sluggish and sulky. They settled down over coffee to gossip about the ball. Who was the mysterious beauty who had so fascinated the Duke? Though they would never have admitted it, they were seething with jealousy.

Ella said nothing. Instead she slipped down to her basement room and took the little glass slipper from its hiding place under a pile of old scraps. She simply did not know what to make of it all.

eanwhile the Duke wandered restlessly through the gardens of the villa. He looked at the glass slipper and sighed. He had been accustomed to the company of the most charming ladies in Europe but none had touched his heart like the stranger who had so enchanted him at the ball.

'I must find her!' he whispered.

Right away he set out to search for the girl who had worn the glass slipper. He visited every street, every house in town. But wherever he went, no lady's foot quite fitted. He began to despair.

Finally he arrived at Mr Cinders' dress shop. Madame Renée and her daughters were all agog to receive such a distinguished guest. When he explained his visit Ruby and Pearl quite forgot themselves and pushed forward eagerly, jostling one another in a very undignified manner.

With a great deal of fuss and bother and fluttering of eyelashes they vied to try on the glass slipper, first Ruby, then Pearl. But though they both pushed and shoved and pleaded and squashed up their toes, it was no use. The slipper simply did not fit.

Madame Renée, who had been peering intently over their shoulders like a beady-eyed blackbird trying to capture a worm, could hardly contain her rage and disappointment.

The Duke prepared to leave. Then he noticed a figure standing in the shadows. A servant, surely, he thought, judging by her shabby dress, though there was something about her, something familiar.

'Will you try it?' he asked. The others snorted in amusement. Slowly Ella came forward and sat down.

Of course, the slipper fitted her foot perfectly. There was a gasp of astonishment. And when Ella produced the other matching slipper from her pocket even Madame Renée was stunned into silence.

The Duke took Ella's hand. 'I was afraid I might never see you again,' he said. 'But now I have found you I cannot let you go. Come away with me at once and we will announce our engagement!'

Ella looked around.
She saw that her stepsisters'
faces were ugly with envy
and bad temper. She had
not noticed Buttons. In fact,
she had not noticed him at
all recently because she had
been so taken up with the
glories of the ball. But she
noticed him now.

He was hovering in a corner,
pretending to be busy tying
up a brown paper parcel.

'No,' said Ella slowly.
'Thank you very much,
Duke, but no. I'm sorry –
I can't. You see, I love
someone else.'

At that moment Buttons
looked up at her. And a
bright pink blush of hope
spread up all over his face to
the very tips of his ears.

Mr Cinders started to smile for the first time in a long while. And when his wife pinched his arm crossly and hissed, 'Do something!' he merely smiled wider than ever.

Madame Renée took the Duke aside and said, 'Why not consider one of my daughters instead, your grace? Utterly charming, I'm sure you'll agree. And a better class of girl altogether!'

But the Duke shook his head politely and hurried away from the house as fast as he could. Soon, it was rumoured, he had taken off in his private aeroplane to explore the South American jungle and recover from his broken heart.

'You could have been very rich, you know,' Buttons said to Ella when they were alone together at last.

'Dear Buttons, I don't fancy being a grand lady. I just want to be with you,' she replied. 'And anyway, it could get a bit dull doing nothing all day except being dressed up like an expensive doll. We'll go off and start our own little shop and I'll make stunning clothes, more beautiful than anyone has ever seen. And what's more,' she added, 'I'll have first pick of them.'

'When we are married,' said Buttons, 'you may not live like a duchess but you will eat like a queen. You never did try my bacon and eggs, did you?'

So off they went, with Ella on the crossbar of the bicycle, wobbling a bit because they were laughing so much, and the old grey cat in the basket. It was a lot more fun than being in the back of a limousine.

They were too happy to notice a lady walking alone further up the street, carrying a fancy umbrella. She paused to watch them go. Then, smiling a secret smile, she walked on.

For Alice

The artwork for this book was done in gouache
colour combined with pen line.
The ball scenes were inspired by the dance sequences
in the R.K.O. Fred Astaire/Ginger Rogers movies.
The dresses are my designs, inspired by the great French
couturiers of the 1920s such as Doucet, Poiret and Patou.

Shirley Hughes

ELLA'S BIG CHANCE
A BODLEY HEAD BOOK 0 370 32765 9
Published in Great Britain by The Bodley Head, an imprint of Random House Children's Books. This edition published 2003
3 5 7 9 10 8 6 4 2
The Random House Group Ltd Reg. No. 954009.
Printed in China. A CIP catalogue record for this book is available from the British Library.
RANDOM HOUSE CHILDREN'S BOOKS 61–63 Uxbridge Rd, London W5 5SA. A division of The Random House Group Ltd